MR. MUD go SCHOOL

by Roger Hargreaves

Copyright© 1980, 1982 by Roger Hargreaves
Published in U.S.A. by Price/Stern/Sloan Publishers, Inc.
410 North La Cienega Boulevard, Los Angeles, California 90048
Printed in U.S.A. All Rights Reserved.
ISBN: 0-8431-1104-6

PRICE/STERN/SLOAN
Publishers, Inc., Los Angeles
1983

BE WISE

Have you ever met a man like Mr. Muddle?
Mr. Muddle does everything in a muddle.
Just look at the way he built his house.

2

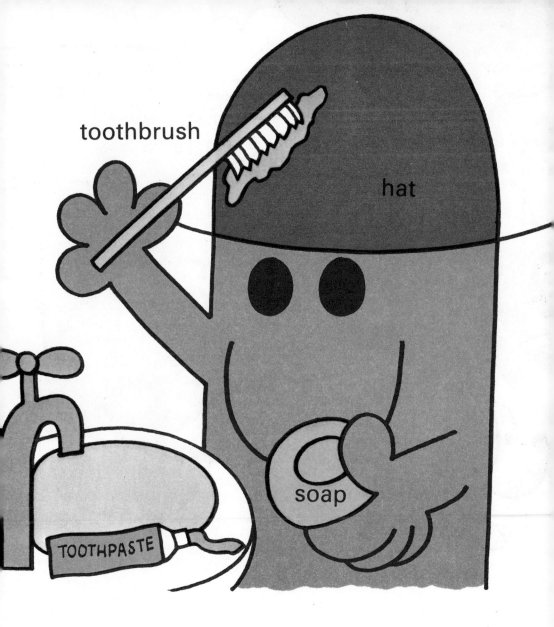

toothbrush

hat

soap

TOOTHPASTE

Mr. Muddle can get into a muddle just brushing his teeth. Mr. Muddle puts soap on his toothbrush. Then he brushes his hat.

tree

car

dog

One day, Mr. Muddle met his clever friend, Mr. Clever. "Good morning," said Mr. Clever. "Good evening," said Mr. Muddle.

house

sun

SCHOOL BUS

Mr. Clever

"Oh, dear, you are in a muddle," said Mr. Clever. "You should go to school. I am sure the teacher could help you, Mr. Muddle."

5

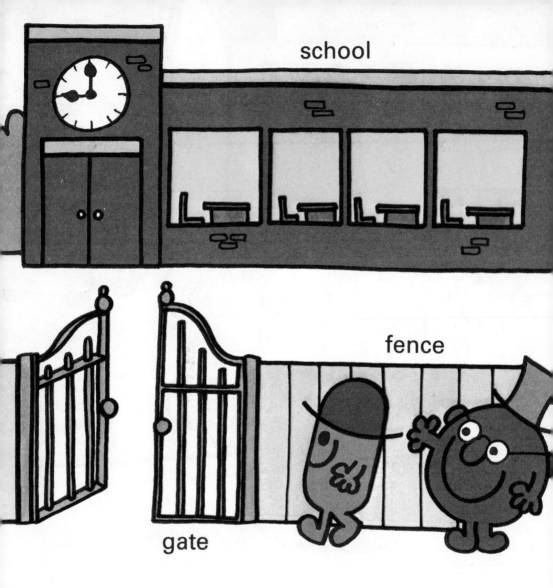

school

fence

gate

Mr. Muddle thought that going to school
was a good idea. "I'll go yesterday," he said.
"I think you mean today," laughed Mr.
Clever.

6

ball

boy

girl

So Mr. Muddle went to school. He met some children in the school playground. "Come into school with us, Mr. Muddle," they said.

blackboard

door

teacher

The children took Mr. Muddle along to the classroom. "Hello, Mr. Muddle," said the teacher. "Goodbye," said Mr. Muddle.

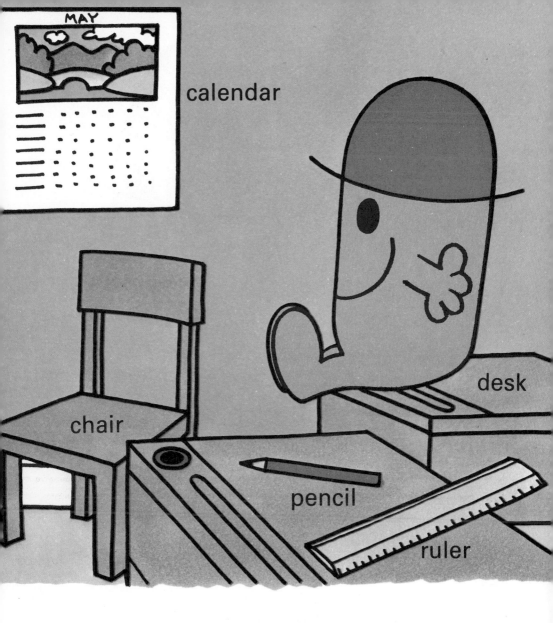

calendar

desk

chair

pencil

ruler

The teacher was very kind. "Come and sit on this chair," she said. "Thank you," said Mr. Muddle. And he sat on the desk.

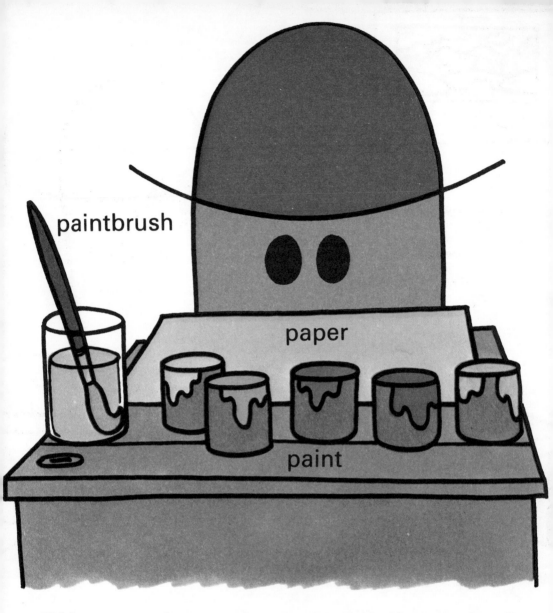

paintbrush

paper

paint

"We are going to do some painting today,"
said the teacher. She gave Mr. Muddle a
paintbrush and some cans of paint.

picture

easel

stool

Just look at Mr. Muddle's picture. He has
painted a lion with a tiger's head. The tiger
has a rabbit's tail. What a muddle.

custard

knife

lamb chop

glass

spoon

At lunchtime, Mr. Muddle got things very muddled. He poured custard on his lamb chop. Then he tried to slice the gravy.

"Oh, Mr. Muddle," cried the teacher. "We must do something about your muddles. Now, I think I have an idea . . ." she said.

flower

bookcase

vase

desk

chair

After lunch, the teacher tried out her new idea. "Just sit on this DESK please, Mr. Muddle," said the teacher.

map

clock

book

desk

chair

wastepaper basket

Can you guess what happened? Mr. Muddle
sat on the CHAIR. And that was just what
the teacher wanted. Her idea was working.

In the cooking class, Mr. Muddle learned
how to make pie. "Roll out the dough until
it is nice and LUMPY," said the teacher.

dish

jam tarts

JAM

table

So Mr. Muddle rolled out the dough until it was nice and FLAT. "Good," said the teacher. "That is just what I wanted."

goal

soccer player

Later, everyone went outside to play games.
First, Mr. Muddle played soccer. "Kick the
ball AWAY from the goal," said one boy.

whistle

soccer shoe

referee

So Mr. Muddle kicked the ball TOWARDS
the goal. In fact, Mr. Muddle kicked the ball
right INTO the goal and won the game.

rope

hoop

bench

Next, Mr. Muddle played on the playground.
There were all kinds of things to crawl
through and to jump over.

flag

sack

line

box

"Just jump UNDER that box, Mr. Muddle,"
said the teacher. So Mr. Muddle jumped OVER
the box, which was the right thing to do.

school

girl   boy

Then it was time to go home. "You have
done well in school today, Mr. Muddle," said
the teacher. "You may come again
tomorrow."

22

cupboard

rench fries

jello

stove

"Thank you," said Mr. Muddle. Then he
went home and cooked himself a special
supper. Fried jello and french fries. "Oh, Mr.
Muddle."

Can you find these words in this book?

 book

page 15

 bowl

page 16

 calendar

page 9

 chair

page 9

 dog

page 4

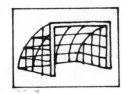 goal

page 18

 jello

page 23

 map

page 15

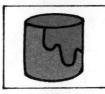 paint

page 10

 referee

page 19

 school

page 6

 toothbrush

page 3